SET 2

Text copyright © Mary Hooper 1966
Illustrations copyright © Allan Curless 1966

First published in Great Britain in 1996
by Macdonald Young Books

Reprinted in 2006 and 2007 by Wayland,
an imprint of Hachette Children's Books

The right of Mary Hooper to be identified as the
author and Allan Curless the illustrator of this
Work has been asserted by them in accordance
with the Copyright, Designs and Patents Act 1988

Designed and Typeset by Backup... Creative Services, Dorset.
Printed in China

British Library Cataloguing in Publication Data
available

ISBN-13: 978 0 7502 5034 4

Wayland
338 Euston Road, London NW1 3 BH
Wayland is an Hachette Livre UK Company

MARY HOOPER

TIME FLIES

Illustrated by Allan Curless

WAYLAND

Chapter One

"I'm not going to like living here," Lucy said with a shiver, and she looked up at the arched ceiling of the vast stairwell with its beams and carved figures. "It's spooky."

"Nonsense," her mum said briskly, pausing to adjust the arm on a suit of armour. "It's different, that's all. It'll soon feel like home."

"Home!" Lucy said. "How can *this* be *home*?"

Lucy's mum had just taken a job as housekeeper in a big Tudor mansion and was busy taking stock of what needed to be

done before it opened to the public. Lucy, meanwhile, was busy wishing herself back in the perfectly ordinary ground-floor flat they'd just left.

"Oh, come on!" Lucy said, for her mum was pausing at every carpet, every window, every step of their journey upstairs. "Let's go and look in the bedrooms."

"It would speed things up if you helped me," her mum said. "You could write labels and stick them on things that need attention. Or you could unpack our kitchen stuff or…"

"Oh, Mum!" Lucy wailed.

"You *are* going to have to help a little more, you know," her mum said, writing something on a clipboard. "It'll be fun living here, but it'll mean some hard work."

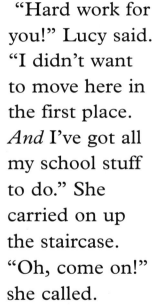

"Hard work for you!" Lucy said. "I didn't want to move here in the first place. *And* I've got all my school stuff to do." She carried on up the staircase. "Oh, come on!" she called.

Her mum was still writing and didn't reply, so Lucy went further up the stairs. At the top there was a hallway as long as a ballroom, with a line of closed doors down each side.

Lucy shivered again: how secretive and forbidding the doors looked – as if each held some dreadful mystery.

But that was stupid, she told herself sternly. They were only *doors*. She took a deep breath, pushed open the first one and went in.

Musty, fusty, dusty! she thought. It was softly dark in there, but she could see a vast four-poster bed hung about with drapes. There were dreary tapestries hanging from the walls and sagging velvet curtains at the windows. Where a shaft of sunlight came through a tear in the curtains, the dust, disturbed by the opening of the door, rose and swirled.

Lucy pulled a face. How *grotty*. From outside the room she heard her mum, voice rather muffled, call, "Coming!"

Lucy decided to hide. If nothing else, she thought, the house should be good for hide and seek.

She could have gone behind a wall hanging, or under the four-poster, but instead she chose a large oak box standing at the bottom of the bed. It was carved with fruits and leaves and strange plants, and had the Latin words *Tempus Fugit* on the top.

Tempus Fugit

"Time flies," Lucy murmured, for the same words were written on the old sundial in the garden, and her mum had told her what they meant.

She lifted the lid of the box, slipped inside and closed it behind her. It was big

enough to take her lying full length, and so
deep that when she lifted her arms she
could only just touch the top.

She breathed in deeply and almost
coughed at the strange smells: a mixture of
moth balls, spices, age-old dust and
something else, something high and sweet
and unknown.

Lucy felt a moment's panic. It's like a
coffin in here, she thought, and was
relieved when, a moment later, she heard
her mum come into the room.

"Surprise!" she cried, sitting up and
flinging open the lid.

But it was Lucy who got the surprise…

Chapter Two

The first thing she noticed was the torches: two of them, flaming brightly on the wall each side of the bed. Next there was the bed itself, which was covered in a heavy fabric, patterned all over with leaves and flowers. She drew in her breath sharply – and then her attention was drawn to the tapestries hanging on the walls, which were

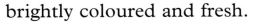

brightly coloured and fresh.
There were paintings on the walls, too, and heavy wooden shutters on each side of the windows. It was the same room... and yet a *different* room.

Lucy gripped the sides of the box. What on earth was happening? Was she dreaming? But the box was hard and real under her fingers, and when she bit her lip she felt real pain.

Crash! Lucy almost died of fright as, with an enormous clang, a warming pan crashed down heavily onto the side of the box.

Terrified, she wheeled round and found herself staring into the eyes of a stout woman with a fierce, red face.

"How dare you!" the woman said. "I never saw such a thing in all my life!"

Lucy just sat there, too scared to move or even blink.

"Get downstairs!" the woman roared. "What do you think you're doing in the Master's bedroom?"

"I didn't... I was..." Lucy stuttered.

The woman hauled her out. "Such goings on! No kitchen skivvy is allowed upstairs! You know that!"

"P... please..." Lucy began.

Unwillingly, Lucy was dragged across the room. "Get back into the kitchen and tell Mistress King that she's not to let her staff wander!"

Lucy hesitated, terrified and reluctant to leave the box, but the woman pushed her towards the top of the stairs.

"Get you down!" she gestured, poking Lucy with every word. "Master's coming tonight. If the house isn't ready for him we'll all feel the hard end of his stick!"

Fearing that she'd be pushed down if she didn't move, Lucy began to stumble down

the stairs. Bewildered and frightened, she looked about her. Everything was different: everything was changed. Bright tapestries hung above her, the oak stairs were light-coloured and polished, torches flamed from the walls. The only thing that hadn't changed was the suit of armour, which was standing in the same place on the bend of the stairs.

But what could have happened? Trembling, Lucy stretched out her arms and looked down at herself. She seemed the same, real and substantial; she wasn't a ghost. She caught sight of her reflection in one of the portraits. She was wearing the same clothes she'd put on that morning: a scruffy black skirt and old tee-shirt that had seemed good enough for exploring a dusty old house.

But the house wasn't dusty any more. It wasn't old, either. Everything was new. Almost... Lucy's heart started beating very fast... almost as if she was back in Tudor times.

Chapter Three

Lucy carried on to the bottom of the stairs. She felt as if she was in a nightmare – either that or the crazy house at the fair. Everything seemed out of focus, tilted, unreal. It wasn't happening... surely it wasn't happening...?

But it was. People hurried along the corridor downstairs, carrying wood or coal or plates or utensils. A maid in a spotless white apron and lace cap passed with what looked like a pile of sheets; two young boys walked by, straining under the weight of a cauldron of water; a tall, thin man hurried along with a sheaf of papers under his arm.

"Come on! Come on!" A woman in a greasy black dress gave Lucy a shove. "You're one of the new ones, aren't you? How did you get out of the kitchen?"

Lucy stumbled towards where the kitchen was – where, just a short while ago, she'd been sitting having a bowl of cereal. When she pushed what she thought was the kitchen door, though, it opened onto nothing but fields and fresh air.

"What are you playing at?" the same woman roared, and before Lucy could even think about running out, she hauled her back and slammed the door. "Get to the kitchen, girl! You stupid or something?"

Lucy was shoved again and staggered along another corridor. *Of course,* she thought as she half-ran, half-stumbled along. The kitchen she'd been in at breakfast time had been a new one. It wasn't built now. Whenever *now* was…

She came to a vast room, like a barn, with a fire at each end and stone walls which ran with condensation. All was heat and chaos and confusion:

people shouted at each other, screamed, crashed plates, dropped things, chopped vegetables, sliced meat and hammered at bones. In one of the fireplaces a great ox was slowly revolving on a spit before a roaring fire, in the other a black cauldron bubbled. Lucy put her hands over her ears. She wanted to cry but felt as if she didn't have any breath to do so.

"You! In the scullery!" Lucy was pushed into a cave-like room off the central one. "Get an apron on and start cleaning those pans!"

The door was slammed behind Lucy and she drew a deep breath and leant on it for a moment. Things were out of control. She felt she wanted to stop, put her head in her hands and go over, minute by weird minute, everything that had happened. Perhaps if she could just stop and think she'd be able to make sense of everything…

"You'll have to go for more water," a voice said, and Lucy noticed a small, slight girl almost hidden behind a sink piled with saucepans, pewter dishes, plates and basins. "We have to draw it up from the well ourselves."

"But I don't know... I don't understand..."

"The well is in the centre courtyard," the girl said. "There's an apron behind you. Best look lively – Mistress King beat me black and blue last week when I didn't get on quickly enough."

"But what's happening?" Lucy stammered.

"Master is coming, that's what. Master is coming and there's a banquet tonight."

"Who... who's Master?" Lucy asked.

"The Earl of Arvon," said the girl. "Don't you even know that? The banquet's to celebrate his return from a journey to the Americas."

"What's he like?" Lucy asked.

The girl shuddered. "I've only seen him once but that was enough – he's big and fierce as a giant, with black eyes that look

right through you. I thought him a brute, but they say he's one of the favourites of our sovereign queen."

"Sovereign queen?" Lucy faltered.

"Our most gracious Queen Elizabeth, of course," said the girl. "Now get on and get the water!"

Chapter Four

It was dusk. Lucy only knew this because the light in the scullery had grown dimmer and dimmer until her new friend, Ellen, had gone outside to beg for a scrap of a candle so that they could see.

The mountain of dishes hadn't grown any smaller, for almost as soon as they were washed they were replaced by others. Lucy felt heavy with tiredness; her back ached and her hands were raw, the fingertips bleeding.

"Will there be much more?" she gasped, as one of the men-servants brought in yet another pile.

"Aye," Ellen said. "We'll be here until midnight at least. Master's feeding over two hundred tonight."

"But I can't… I've got to…" Lucy began, tears starting in her eyes. But how could she explain? She didn't even believe it herself.

There was a noise and commotion from outside and the door suddenly crashed open.

"I want you!" Mistress King roared, pointing at Lucy.

Frightened, Lucy went out. She was

hauled towards the vast fireplace and prodded until she was standing, hot coals crunching under her feet, almost in the fire.

"The boy's fainted, so you're to take over turning the ox. And if you stop, or let it burn, it'll be the worse for you!"

The turning handle on the spit was so hot it burnt Lucy's hands and the heat from the roaring fire scorched her face, but she did as she was told. After only a few moments, though, she found it almost impossible to carry on. It was unbearably hot, she didn't have the strength necessary to turn the heavy beast and her back felt as if it was breaking.

She began to cry, then sob, but no one took the slightest bit of notice. Feeling more wretched than she'd ever felt in her life before, Lucy realised that no one was going to help her. If she was going to get away, then she'd have to work things out for herself.

She wiped her eyes on the rough

linen apron, then looked around her. The kitchens were still chaotic and frenzied. So frenzied, she decided, that if she disappeared no one would notice she'd gone – at least for a moment or two.

She left the fireplace and slipped, silent as a shadow, through the huddle of people and towards one of the doors. Letting herself out she fled along a corridor, desperately trying to remember which way she'd come.

She took a left turn and then a right, down a hallway and up some back stairs. At last she came to the long row of bedroom doors she'd been looking for. Panting with fear, she ran on, not caring now whether she was seen or not.

Just as she reached the end bedroom, the door opposite opened and a man dressed in a richly coloured Tudor costume strode out. He was big and brutish – like an ogre, Lucy thought. His face was fierce and unpleasant enough, but it was his eyes which made her shudder with fear, for they were deep and penetrating, overshadowed by thick brows. She stared into them as if hypnotised, too terrified to move.

"Who are you?" he roared, making a lunge for Lucy. He gripped her arm, reaching for his sword with his other hand.

"How dare a servant enter my quarters!"

Lucy gave a sob of terror and, knowing that if she didn't get away now then she'd *never* make it, she managed to break from his gaze and wriggle away. She threw herself at the door opposite. It opened immediately and she flew across the room, lifted the lid of the chest and fell into it.

There was the same high, sweet smell and – something Lucy hadn't noticed before – a sensation of falling.

Sick with fear, she counted to ten, then lifted the lid.

"There you are!" said her mum. "Thought you'd play a trick on me, did you?"

Chapter Five

Lucy sat still for a moment, stunned and breathless. Slowly she looked around the bedroom. It was all right: the tapestries were dark, the curtains were torn, the bed covering was old and threadbare.

"I'm back," she breathed, and wanted to cry with relief.

Her mum smiled. "Where have you been, then?"

"I know this is – well…" Lucy bit her lip. "I think I've been back in Tudor times."

"Well, you weren't very long!" her mum said, amused.

"How… how long have I been in here?" Lucy faltered, climbing out of the chest.

"About a minute."

"But I…"

"You didn't hit your head on the lid, did you?" her mum said. "I think you've been dreaming!"

"But it was... all different. Torches and tapestries, and there was a different bedspread, and..."

"Yes, all this will have to be replaced," her mum said, scribbling rapidly. "The

fabric will never stand a hundred visitors a day touching it."

"But you don't..."

"Darling, would you go and get my long tape measure?" said her mum. "I think it's in one of the boxes."

"No, I..." Lucy began, and then she had a sudden vision of the scullery and the deep sink of cold water and the piles of greasy cooking tins. "Okay," she said.

Her legs were still shaking as she walked down the staircase. She *must* have dreamed it. She couldn't possibly... it just couldn't happen...

Suddenly she stopped by the suit of armour, staring, horrified, at the portrait which hung above it.

It was a man in Tudor costume. An ogre of a man with heavy bushy brows over fierce, penetrating eyes which stared down at Lucy menacingly.

A small sign underneath said: *The Earl of Arvon, painted at a banquet to celebrate his return from the Americas, 1596.*

If you have enjoyed this book, why not try these other creepy titles:

The Claygate Hound by Jan Dean
It's the school trip to Claygate, and Zeb and Ryan are ready
to explore, until they hear stories about the ghost in the
woods. It all sounds like a stupid story. But then the boys
start to see shadows moving in the trees and eyes glistening
in the darkness. Could the Claygate Hound really exist?

The Ghosts of Golfhawk School by Tessa Potter
Martin and Dan like to scare others with stories about the
ghosts at Golfhawk School. But when Kirsty arrives and
strange things start to happen it no longer seems a joke.
Can she really see ghostly figures in the playground? And
why have students and teachers started to get sick?

Beware the Wicked Web by Anthony Masters
Where had the enormous, dusty spider's web come from?
The sticky, silky folds had filled the attic room, and were
now clinging to Rob and Sam as they explored the room.
In the centre of the web was a huge egg, which was just
about to hatch…

Danny and the Sea of Darkness by David Clayton
When does a dream become reality? Danny wakes one
night to find himself out at sea during a terrible storm. As
he falls overboard into the icy water Danny wonders if he
will ever return from the Sea of Darkness.

Ghost on the Landing by Eleanor Allen
Jack wakes in the night screaming in fear. His sister's ghost
stories about Aunt Stella's spooky old house must have
been giving him nightmares. But was it just a bad dream or
does the ghost on the landing really exist?